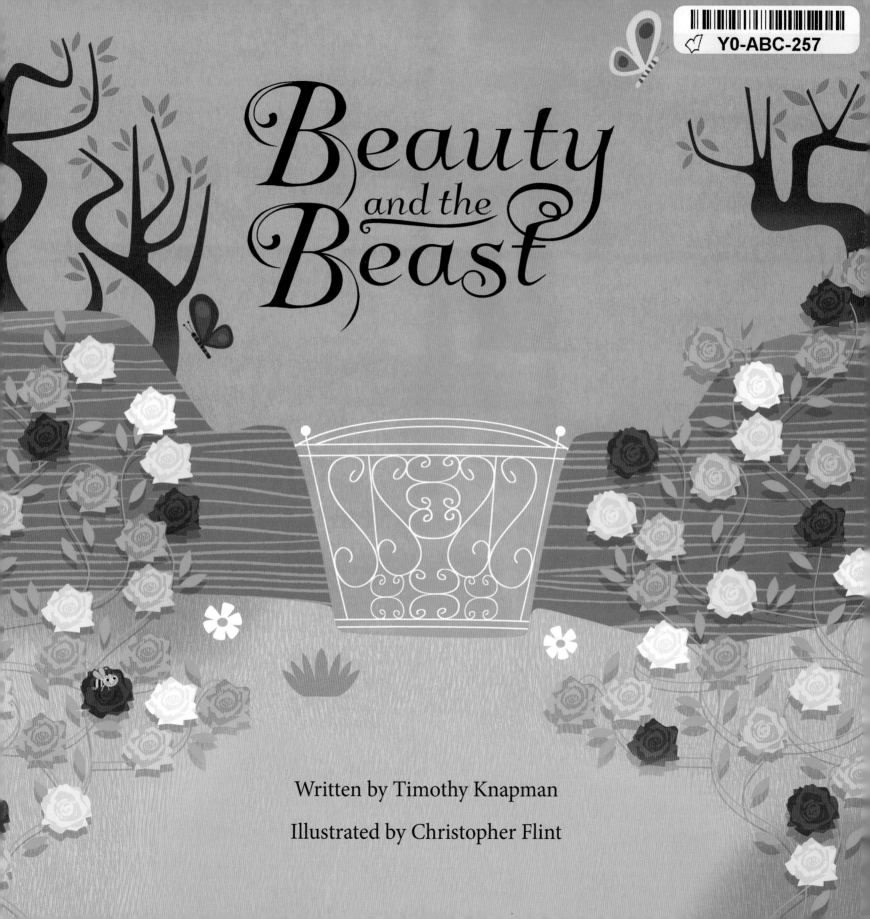

Beauty
and the
Beast

Written by Timothy Knapman

Illustrated by Christopher Flint

There once was a girl named Beauty,
as kind as she was pretty, who liked
to read books and dreamt of adventure.

Beauty's father was poor but hardworking, and
he loved his daughter more than anything.

One day, Beauty's father set off to find work in the city, but before he left he asked his beloved daughter if she would like a special gift when he returned.

Beauty didn't want to trouble him, so she asked for a simple thing. "Why don't you bring me back a rose, Father?" And he promised he would.

But on his way to the city, Beauty's father got lost in
a thick, dark forest where the wind howled, thunder
rumbled, and lightning flashed across the sky.

In the midst of the storm, he came
across a strange and beautiful castle,
overgrown with rose briars.

The roses reminded him of his promise
to Beauty. Just as he was about to pluck
the prettiest rose from the castle walls…

...a monstrous Beast appeared and cried,

"HOW DARE YOU STEAL FROM ME!"

"I'm sorry!" said Beauty's father, shivering in his tired old boots. "I didn't mean to steal! The rose was a gift for my daughter. Please let me go!" he begged.

"I'll let you go...if you promise to send your daughter to me!" growled the Beast.

"I promise," said Beauty's terrified father.

When Beauty's father made it back home, he thought his daughter would be upset at the promise he had made, but Beauty would do anything to protect her family.

Besides, it sounded like the kind of adventure she had read about in one of her books!

When Beauty eventually arrived at the castle, the Beast was waiting for her at the gate.

He looked scary, but Beauty thought he just wanted company. He seemed lonely.

The Beast showed Beauty around his magical and beautiful castle.

He led her through a grand ballroom...

and into a wonderful library full of books.

Upstairs, the Beast had prepared a bedroom for Beauty
to stay in, with a closet full of the prettiest dresses.
The Beast wanted Beauty to be happy in his castle.

Every morning, Beauty and the Beast would
find new books to read in the library.

Every afternoon, they would walk in the garden, and the Beast would pick the prettiest rose he could find for her.

Every night, they would dance in the grand ballroom.
Round and round and round they danced, until Beauty
became dizzy with joy.

Beauty grew to care for the Beast
and realized he was good and kind.

She had never been so happy, but she often thought of
her father and wondered when she would see him again.

The Beast, who didn't want to see her worry, let her visit her father under the condition that she return after one week.

He was falling in love with Beauty, and could not bear to be parted from her for too long.

The Beast gave Beauty a magic ring. "If you're ever missing someone you love, just make a wish," he said. "This ring will reunite you with them."

When Beauty returned home, her father was so happy to see her. "My darling daughter, you're alive!" he cried. "I was terrified of what that frightening Beast had done with you."

"But Father, he's not frightening at all," said Beauty, remembering the Beast's friendship. "He is...he's not what you think."

Days passed and life returned to normal, but Beauty missed the Beast and wanted to return to the castle.

"Soon," said her father, "but not today, I beg you."

Before long, a week had passed…she'd broken her promise!
That very night she had a nightmare that the Beast was dying.

Beauty woke up in tears, realizing his heart
was breaking because she hadn't returned.

"My poor Beast!" cried Beauty. "I must go back to him before it's too late." She used the magic ring to return to the castle and to her love.

When Beauty
reached
the castle,

she went running
through all of the rooms
searching for the Beast.

She found him in the garden, looking weak and very sad.
She burst into tears.

"You must not die!" she cried.
"I cannot live without you. I love you!"

As Beauty's tears fell on the Beast,
there came a flash of light,
and the Beast magically transformed
into a handsome prince!

"At last I am free!" he said. "Many years ago, a wicked witch turned me into a terrifying Beast, but your love for me has broken the spell."

"Will you marry me, Beauty?"
"Of course I will!" Beauty exclaimed.

Beauty's father came to live in the castle and tended to the roses.

As for Beauty and her Prince…they lived happily ever after,
and every night they danced until they were dizzy with joy.

Quarto is the authority on a wide range of topics.

Quarto educates, entertains and enriches the lives of our readers—enthusiasts and lovers of hands-on living.

www.quartoknows.com

Copyright © QEB Publishing, Inc. 2017

Published in the United States in 2017 by QEB Publishing
Part of The Quarto Group
6 Orchard, Lake Forest, CA 92630

Written by Timothy Knapman
Illustrated by Christopher Flint

A CIP record for this book is available from the Library of Congress.

ISBN: 978-1-68297-211-3

Printed in China